DEDICATED TO MY MOTHER—

WHO ALWAYS ENCOURAGED MY INNER WITCH

1

Secret Tapes

"You can't go off to battle and leave me here to wonder if you're coming back," my voice broke on the last word.

"I have no choice, my love," was the sad reply. "It is my duty."

A tear slid down my cheek, dripping from my chin to the floor. I hastily wiped at my eye. "I won't stay behind. I refuse."

"You won't be any help to us. You'd just slow us down."

"Because you're out of shape," a hushed whisper came from my right.

"And a woman." Two sets of giggles and a snort followed.

The red light I'd been staring at stopped blinking. "And, *cut!*" Sruthi called. The bedroom came back into focus, hazy afternoon sun slanted across the bed in front of me where my best friend sat, aiming a camera at my face.

I rubbed the dampness from my face and rolled my eyes. I turned around in my seat to glare at my sister and one of my best friends. "You're totally killing my concentration, Kennedy. Eva, *don't* egg her on. Sruthi and I can shoot these scenes alone if necessary."

Kennedy snorted again. "Sorry, sis. It was too good of an opportunity to miss." Bangles rattled against her wrist as she spoke.

"Yeah Anastasia, why'd you pick such a misogynistic piece to audition with?" Eva quipped at me. We were shooting an audition tape for UCLA in Sruthi's bohemian bedroom. I preferred it for two reasons; her cream bedroom wall was the perfect backdrop, and my mom was so against the thought of me professionally acting that I had to keep these tapes a secret.

"They only gave us two choices," I explained with a sigh, "and the other one was *comedy*." My nose wrinkled as I spoke. "Mirror me."

Kennedy passed over a handheld mirror so I could re-apply my eye makeup and smooth my chambray shirt collar. My soft, natural curls were styled in an afro and pinned back on one side of my head to create an edgier look. Bold winged eyeliner made my deep brown eyes pop. My huge, pearly smile- the feature I hoped would get me into Hollywood- beamed back at me. It contrasted against the beautiful, dark skin my family shared. I started exercising the muscles in my face before we shot the scene again, opening and closing my eyes and mouth, and I could see Kennedy mocking me from behind in the glass. With a smirk, I tossed the mirror back to her. But before it could hit her, she flicked out her right wrist and it froze in midair.

Oh, yeah. Did I mention we're witches?

Pause.

The four of us are part of a medium sized coven of witches and warlocks in southern Oregon that stay off the grid. After all, folks haven't taken to us all that well in the past. Covens across the world generally keep to themselves for peace and safety through protective charms and invisibility shields. You see, there was never really a time where it was socially acceptable to be a witch. I mean, it goes back past Joan of Arc really.

With a chuckle, my sister reached out and pulled the mirror from midair with thin, pink-tipped fingers. At sixteen, she was short and thin, nearly a head below me. Bright and bubbly, but also mischievous and hilarious, she was a little ball of sunshine. Her natural curls hung to her shoulders, and were pushed back with a tribal design headband. "Too fast for you," Ken crowed, laughing. Her dark skin was accentuated by the plain white t-shirt she wore, a bright yellow pendant, and her favorite pink eye-shadow.

"Okay, well, switch it up a bit," Eva suggested, twisting her short brown hair around her finger. "Try giving your character a little more backbone. A little more... *fuego*."

"That one means fire," Kennedy informed us. Eva was teaching her Spanish.

I straightened my spine and lifted my chin. "*Fuego*, comin' right up."

"Also, while we're taking suggestions, I'm getting hungry," Eva whined.

"Alright, let's shoot this scene again, and then we'll make food," Sruthi said softly in her lilting English accent. Her dark hair cascaded across her face, and she pushed it back with both hands. "Don't mess it up this time?" she suggested pointedly with an eyebrow raised.

My sister made a show of locking her lips and sitting on her hands, smiling at Sruthi out of the corner of her eyes. Eva grinned and curled her lilac cloak up in her lap with her witch's hat.

Seventeen and pretty, Eva had dainty Puerto Rican features and smooth honey-tinted skin. She kept her hair in a short, angled lob.

"Alright. I want to shoot it from a different angle, and we'll mesh the two clips together. Like Eva said, this time focus less on how heartbroken you are and try giving me a little more rebellion," Sruthi suggested. As someone who wanted to work in film and media, she was the perfect director for my auditions.

"Got it," I nodded, lifting my chin. "Rebellion is my specialty."

"And, *action!*"

I blew into a steaming cup of lavender tea as I sat cross-legged on Sruthi's bed the following afternoon. Eva was at home journaling and doing yoga, and Kennedy was watching a movie with my mom.

"Strength doesn't always require a sword," Sruthi murmured.

"Huh?" I nearly choked as I looked up from her computer. "That's deep."

She giggled. "No, dummy. I was reading the tea bag." Her thin fingers held it up.

"*Oh.* Oh, duh. I thought you were just being a philosophical Taurus. Mine says, 'Keep your chin up.'" I jutted my chin into the air and Sruthi snorted.

We'd been sitting in comfortable silence since Sruthi had brought the tea in. I was reading a short screenplay she'd written on tree fairies and conserving forests while she edited the self-tape we'd filmed earlier. Her work was brilliant and I was beyond excited to start shooting it. Sruthi was planning to enter it into festivals around the country and abroad.

"I really like this part here about telling the humans they wouldn't exist without the trees. That there would be no home for them to destroy the earth from."

"Hmm? Oh, me too," she said softly, but there was steel in her tone and flames in her eyes. "I have to spell out the irony for them, it seems."

I took another sip of tea and sighed. "If anyone can spell it out for them, it's you, Sruth." I tapped the bottom of the mug with my finger, and a few orange sparks shot out, warming my drink.

"Thanks." She smiled. Born to second-generation Pakistani-British parents, Sruthi had long brown hair that hung almost to her waist; hazel eyes that turned up at the edges, which she often decorated with winged eyeliner; a straight, long nose, and arched lips. She was nearly as tall as me, and athletically built, though she had never played a sport in her life. She had changed into silk strawberry-pink pants and a baggy, gray Nancy Drew Detective sweatshirt.

Scattered around her bedroom were books and plants, dozens of each. Bookcases were filled with mystery novels, creased tales of fiction, and thick, dusty, nonfiction volumes. All the stories she had read helped her set up shots and translate thoughts to film. Atop every surface were succulents, little bonsai trees, and flowers as well. Little vines hung from wooden shelves between her windows. Her room was colorful and bright against the light walls.

Sruthi drained her tea and set the mug on her antique bedside table.

"This part here is really good," she murmured, gesturing to my audition. "I think if we switch to the side perspective while you cry and zoom in the tiniest bit, it'll really highlight the emotion of the scene."

"*Dra*-ma," I drawled, and we laughed.

"A little bit of drama, a whole lot of change-the-world."

"And maybe a dash of fame?" I suggested, grinning.

Our love for film-making had brought us close. I had always thought of acting as a way to step outside of the limitations being a witch placed on me. Per coven rules, I wasn't allowed to interact with regular humans or explore the outer world. But stepping into characters let me do that. Sruthi had a similar mind-set; she felt that her views and usefulness to Mother Earth were restricted inside of the coven, and that by making documentaries and short films she could spread her message. We had been working together for over a year, but the coven had specific rules about contact with the outside world.

2
Kill Joy

Like most fall evenings in Crater Lake National Park, the sky grew dark early that night and a heavy fog rolled over the water. These were my favorite nights, when I felt most like myself as I walked down familiar paths lit only by crisp moonlight. My pointed, black, over-the-knee boots crunched along loose rocks as I headed through the woods along my coven's base camp. A thick burgundy cape billowed out behind me, keeping me cozy. My familiar, Dezi, trotted ahead of me, chasing some unseen bug. Her sleek black fur glimmered in the moonlight and her tail flicked. I named her Desiree when we first met, but she was so edgy and sassy that shortening it fit her even better. She definitely never seemed to care what I called her; or even pretended to hear.

Just before the first houses would come into view, I came to a stop on the forest path and breathed the dusk in deeply. It smelled of earth, of vines, and pine needles. I tilted my face upwards and let the last gray light kiss my cheeks. The moon and stars were just beginning to glimmer through the clouds.

"Thank you," I whispered to the dark sky. No matter what challenges faced me, inside or outside of the coven, I knew I was lucky to walk along this beautiful path guided by stars eons old. I took another deep breath and started traipsing along through the woods again. As the sun went to sleep, the sweet yellow, burnt orange, and deep red leaves around me all faded to dark shades of gray. Sticks and debris crunched under my boots and hints of smoke cloyed at the air as I broke through the tree line. Shrill laughter pierced the night ahead as I approached camp.

I'd just finished editing my audition tape with Sruthi, and she'd e-mailed me a copy to turn in with the rest of my application. *Yes*, witches used e-mail too. We'd spent the past two days shooting the three scenes; the first involved me discussing my love and sadness when my anonymous partner went off to war, the second was an internal battle where I decided to follow them, and the third was me showing up to battle armed with a bow and arrow and a fierce attitude. The third was definitely the most fun to act out. Eva had stood at the edge of the lake with the camera while Sruthi called out directions from beside her, and my sister did touch-ups and made sound effects. Sruthi had me stride out of the forest line with the bow and arrow slung across my back and a determined look on my face right as the sun kissed my skin. I knew from editing how beautiful the shot had turned out and I couldn't wait for UCLA to see it too.

Wondering where my sister and mother were, I snapped my long fingers and a small, rusty orange orb levitated an inch above my palm. I glanced into it and saw them both in our cabin. And it looked like I was almost late for dinner; it was after six. *Shoot.* Anxiety rippled through my stomach; my plan was to confront my mother again now that I'd finished my audition tape. We'd been having an argument about going away to college, and I thought that her watching the tape would help her see my dedication and talent and finally convince her to let me go. I snapped my slim brown fingers again, and my orb disappeared, taking the image with it.

All along the paths, small girls in witches' hats ran back and forth nearby, shrieking and squealing, innocent to the conflicts that came with growing up. Little bursts of color exploded around them like fairy dust as they played. Two teenage boys lounged against a large cabin to my right, dressed in black velvet warlocks' robes, murmuring to each other. Cats sauntered aimlessly. When I came upon a fork in the path, I headed right, and soon our wooden home came into view. Tiny white sparks bounced and danced in the windows- my little sister's favorite trick. My cat kept up, because it was dinnertime.

"Anastasiaaa!" my mother chastised as I opened the door, "You said you would be home nearly an hour ago." The sound of crickets chirping died as I ducked inside and shut the door.

I pulled off my witch's hat and hung it on the coat rack. Little amber gems sewn into it danced in the light and flashed at me as I kicked my boots off. "Sorry, Mama. I lost track of time again." I caught a glimpse of myself in the mirror hung against the wood paneling. I had inherited my high cheekbones and piercing almond eyes from my mother, but my wide nose and pretty, thick lips came from my dad. A delicate, ember pendant rested against my tunic, which hung loosely over leggings. I didn't look like the usual actresses in movies, and I definitely didn't meet Hollywood's typical blonde and blue-eyed beauty standards. But there was something raw and regal about my face that I knew millions of other girls could relate to. If I could just get in front of a talent scout, I was sure they would see it too.

I walked over and joined my mom and sister at the table. "I was spending time with Sruthi," I explained, leaning back against my hands to crack my spine before sitting down. "She's been having a hard time after breaking up with her girlfriend, even if she won't outright admit it. Instead she just obsesses over her plants. We spent the whole day in her greenhouse," I groaned. The girl's green thumb could get a little excessive, but we'd actually spent the afternoon in front of a computer that definitely sat on a desk surrounded by potted plants. I just wasn't ready to broach the subject of my audition tape yet. Kennedy's eyes smiled at my lie, but my palms felt damp at my sides.

My mom shot me a sympathetic smile. The table was bathed in candlelight, and steam from fresh vegetable soup twirled dreamily towards the ceiling. My mother broke apart a loaf of bread, and handed my sister and I pieces absent-mindedly. The candlelight made her skin glow like black silk. "Poor Sruthi. Invite her over soon. She's always welcome here," my mom said.

"Always welcome to tend to your *garden*," I teased, and Kennedy burst out laughing. My mother couldn't keep a plant alive if her life depended on it and our front vegetable patch was the laughing stock of the neighbors. Which was funny, since she was a surgeon and was supposed to keep things...alive.

My mom ignored me and gestured to the soup. "This is from the new cauldron. Tell me if you taste a difference."

"It smells amazing, Mama," Kennedy crowed. "I don't know how you always come up with such good recipes." Most people would think my little sister was a suck-up, but truthfully, she was the most genuine person in my life and one of my best friends. When she wasn't teasing or playing practical jokes, she was kind and sweet and pure and warm. It was fitting that *her* orb was a bright yellow.

"Well, it's not easy to keep two ravenous children satisfied with the same thing, over and over," my mother smirked, sinking into her seat. "But Ken did peel all of the potatoes and carrots."

"Thanks guys," I grinned.

"Oh, I forgot the spoons…" Kennedy started to get up, but my mom smiled at her mischievously.

"I know I always tell you girls not to use your powers out of laziness, but I think we'll make an exception tonight." Her brown eyes glittered as she flicked her long fingers, and three wooden spoons came soaring out of the kitchen drawer, before landing neatly on the table.

"Yes, mama," Kennedy nodded. In turn, she clapped and her glass landed in her hand. She sipped her water conspiratorially, spilling it because she couldn't stop giggling.

"Don't get carried away now!" I joked, digging into the soup. My mom smiled gently.

At fifty-two, she was older than most of the other moms in our coven, but that was because of all the extra school she had to endure to become a certified surgical sorceress, or CSS. She had always told us that she knew we were coming, but that we had to wait until she was good and successful. She carried herself so confidently; head always held high, back straight, and deep eyes warm and knowing. Tonight, she was dressed in a soft red sweater and gray pants. Slight wrinkles lined her face.

To an outsider looking in, this happy scene would appear normal and comfortable. The aroma of steaming vegetables filled the kitchen. Our rustic cabin was bathed in soft light, the sturdy beams were kept spotless by impeccable spell work, and a soft wool blanket lay draped across the couch. Pictures of places my parents had traveled to adorned the walls. It was a safe, peaceful house. For now.

I cleared my throat, ready to talk to my mom while she seemed mellow. I knew what I had to say would rock the boat. I hated to do it, but I had put off the conversation for two days to let her calm down from the last time we had talked about it. Unfortunately, school deadlines didn't wait for over-protective mothers.

After we had all scraped our bowls and patted our stomachs, I picked up our dishes and headed to the kitchen sink, speaking with my back to the table. "Mama, I want to talk to you again. About college." I turned the water on and pointed my finger at the bowls, directing it.

My mother sighed, her brows knitting. "Anastasia, we've been over this," she said slowly. "There's a perfectly good school you can go to with people of your own kind, just like I did."

"I know," I turned around, my hair whipping back. "But that's not what *I* want to do." Without realizing it, I had put both hands on my hips, and the sink water had started shooting everywhere, dousing my chambray tunic. Kennedy stifled a giggle at the table. With an exasperated sigh, I turned it off.

"I already told you, it's too dangerous," my mom replied, shutting her large eyes and leaning back in her chair. Her long braids hung down her back.

Kennedy tensed, expecting another fight to break out. Always the jokester and peacemaker, Ken hated tension. Her eyes started to squint up.

I grimaced. "I'm just asking you again to *think* about it."

"I have thought about it, Ana. Don't you think I thought about it when I decided to become a surgeon?" My mom massaged her forehead. "It's just *too dangerous*. You know what humans are capable of when they learn what we are. You know what hatred they are filled with. There's a perfectly good witchcraft school in Bend with an acting program…" A clock in the living room chimed definitively. My mother was in her element in an operating room, where things were planned out, prepared for, and organized. The world outside the coven was too unexpected and random, and filled her with irrational fear.

"But those witches never make it anywhere!" I whined. I felt a flush creeping up my neck. "When do you ever see them in movies? I want to go to a regular acting school, in New York, or L.A., and make it *big*. I know I can. I've been practicing and performing since I was a child." I glanced beseechingly at my sister.

"Mama, I don't want to get involved, but we really shouldn't stop 'Stasia from following her dreams," Kennedy said hesitantly. "As a woman of color in 2019, she's already got the odds stacked against her if you want to talk about issues like equal pay and representation. Holding her back before she even gets to that point is unfair."

My mother shook her head and met my eyes. "I'm not saying you couldn't make it. I know you could. But life outside of the coven is not meant for us. This is where we stay safe, Anastasia, and I don't want to argue about it anymore. I shouldn't have to keep bringing up Salem to get you to see *sense*," she exhaled angrily.

Eva was a history buff, and she'd schooled us all on witch lore before, so I knew what my mom was referring to. Eva had taught us that a common misconception was that all American witches were hung back in the 1600s in Salem, Massachusetts. However, almost every accused 'witch' was actually just a regular person either suffering from mental illness, charged with not being pious enough, or experiencing hallucinogenic drugs, and it turned into a religious frenzy. Even though for the most part the 'witches' in the Salem trials had been regular humans, we had seen how people acted out of fear and ignorance when they thought their neighbors were magical. Of course, my mom wasn't going to listen to that.

After Salem, our people disbursed throughout the country and went into hiding, even with the knowledge that the victims of the witch trials usually weren't really magic. After all, humans couldn't catch us easily. But when we saw how public opinion was directed towards our kind several American witches and warlocks made deals with the Department of the Interior where we received land in exchange for keeping our society a secret.

Another misunderstanding that Eva taught us about witches was the belief that we were all women and actually part of some matriarchal devil-worshipping society. When in fact it is a pretty even number of witches and warlocks and no, sorry to disappoint; we don't worship the devil and we really aren't all that scary. Being born magic is just something genetic that passes down family lines. Our covens also tend to be very diverse and accepting. They are, however, generally run by males. That's something Kennedy intends to change.

Our hidden covens were something the American public wasn't aware of, and we knew that if they realized we existed, we ran a high risk of losing all the peace our people had worked so hard to achieve. That just wasn't fair to those of us who wanted to branch out of the secret life we'd been forced into.

"I don't even want to be a stupid witch anymore!" I groaned, stalking off to my room. More candlelight danced across the wooden walls as I shut the door behind me. Dezi was nowhere to be found, probably chasing my sister's familiar, Damon, somewhere. Posters of famous women of color actresses were tacked above my desk for inspiration. Little pots and jewelry trays dotted the surfaces of my room. My deep red bedspread looked like the perfect place to lay down and pout.

Okay, I knew I was being a little melodramatic. But look, it's not my fault. I'm an Aquarius. We're passionate, temperamental people. That would actually serve me well in acting school. If my mother would *ever* let me leave the coven and chase my dreams. I twirled a silver ring shaped like vines around my finger restlessly. I figured that once my dad got back from his work trip, I would talk to my parents together and somehow convince them to let me go. I'd been planting the seed and watering it for a while. I flopped onto my bed with a sigh. I knew my mom was mainly worried that I would accidently give myself away as a witch, which was obviously incredibly dangerous for us. But I *was* able to control my magic. That's what all those years of primary witchcraft school had been for. She was just always *so* over-protective. On the other hand, my dad's issue with me leaving was more about appearances. As the Grand Warlock of our coven, there were certain expectations about my sister and I remaining in the coven instead of moving away, taking up positions in our government, and being well-behaved. Three things I was not particularly interested in, if I was being honest.

With a groan, I rolled over in bed and flicked my fingers. The ring on my finger glimmered for a millisecond. My comforting rusty orb appeared above my palm, and I thought about my dad. In seconds, I saw him sitting in a room far away, pouring over paperwork. He had a black cloak on and he looked tense. My dad was on a trip to Florida to meet with the brand new Grand Warlock of another coven in the Keys, which his brother belonged to. Their old Grand Warlock had just passed away, and my father went to investigate the death and lead a passage ceremony for them. My Uncle Ben was a member of that coven, having moved there to get married years before.

Seeing that my dad was too busy to chat about my bright and important future, I snapped my fingers again and changed my focus to one of my other best friends, Eva. I saw her sitting on a couch, flipping through a large book. I touched my orb with my left hand and it appeared in front of her, floating inside of hers. Eva's orb was such a pretty violet. She looked up at me with an eyebrow cocked.

"What's going on?" she asked. "I'm trying to read." Her short brown hair with its natural highlights was messy, and her almond eyes looked tired under thick eyebrows.

"I got in another fight with my mom," I complained, taking a deep breath. I tucked a fluffy pillow under my head and smoothed my curls back. "I'm seriously considering just running away and leaving it all behind so I can star in the next Blockbuster already." I stared at the fake stars I'd bewitched to my ceiling, like non-magic people did with plastic.

"Okay, slow your roll, valley girl," Eva murmured, shutting her large book. The smartest of all my friends, Eva was always the rational one I turned to. Subconsciously, I knew that was why I had reached out to her. I could be a *little* prone to getting carried away and Eva was the problem-solver in my group of friends. "First of all, Blockbuster closed down years ago. So please set a different goal.

Also, you're not running anywhere." She had the slightest accent that came with growing up in a family of first-generation English-speakers.

"I know, I know. I don't really mean it. I think. I'm just so frustrated." I could see my reflection in her orb. My eyes did look a little crazed as I rolled them. "I just want to be a famous actress, is that *so* much to ask?"

"Okay, well, yes," Eva teased. "But you can and you will do it. Just give your parents time to come around to it." She was wearing a hooded black sweatshirt and picking at her manicure as she spoke. "Your dreams will come true. I promise."

I pursed my lips. "I know. You're right. Ugh. It's frustrating because they've known my whole life that I wanted to act. They just didn't realize I wanted to leave to do it." My hammering heart started to slow as she told me what I want to hear. My parents *would* come around. I *would* go to acting school. I *would* be the next big star.

Eva nodded and added, "They can't expect you to stay here forever just because your dad is the Grand Warlock. Your grandpa was, and your dad's brother sure didn't stick around. Plus, I'm always right, *chica*. Can I get back to reading now?" She held her big book up to make a point.

"Good talking to you too!" I muttered sarcastically. "But yeah, fine. Thanks. What are you reading?"

"A book on my old coven's history," Eva said without pause. The walls behind her were a light rose shade and were adorned with posters of French films, palm trees, British boy bands, and popular comics. "I'm still trying to trace my relatives' family trees."

"*Of course* you are," I muttered. Eva was obsessed with ancestry. It made sense, though. When Eva was only four her father had passed away. Her mother moved her and her brother to Oregon because she couldn't deal with the grief of staying in the same country where she had lost her soul-mate. They didn't visit Puerto Rica often, and Eva missed out on a lot of her family history. "Alright, well, I'll see you tomorrow. Hope you learn something interesting."

"Love you, girly."

My orb disappeared and I was alone in my room yet again. The clock on my nightstand said it was only 8:30. Eva was right about one thing: my parents definitely expected me to stick around and follow in my dad's footsteps. But just because something was tradition didn't mean it couldn't be broken. Grand Warlocks are elected for life, unless they step down, and it's typical for the family of the Grand Warlock to stay within the same coven. My Uncle Ben broke that tradition when he married my Aunt Tara, who lived in a Floridian coven. And my grandfather's sister had left when a New York coven had an opening for a transfiguration teacher. So, it wasn't impossible; just against the grain.

I knew my sister was planning to stay in our coven and get into government, just like our parents wanted. But she was doing it for herself. Like me, Kennedy was tired of seeing minorities struggle to get to the top, both in and out of the coven. She wanted to use her voice to influence politics and laws, while I wanted to use mine to tell stories and bring awareness to our plights.

I thought about reaching out to whine to Sruthi but decided to just get ready for bed. I pointed to my dresser and some red and white flannel pajamas soared my way, along with my silver hair bonnet. A satisfied smirk crossed my face, knowing I was using my powers even though my mom would tell me I shouldn't be lazy just because I was a witch. I changed and got under the covers. A few quick finger flicks later, I had a DVD in the player and a movie about female mathematicians came on. Having seen the film a dozen times, I watched less for the plot and more for the acting. I tried to match my facial expressions to the main character's. I pitched my voice like hers and tried to pull deep emotion into it. I wanted to audition for badass roles like this one, where the protagonist wasn't driven by a relationship or saved by a man. She did what she had to do to succeed and she lived by her morals, seeking to better the lives of those around her.

At some point hours later, I must have dozed off.

3

Brave Heart

I woke up in the middle of the night to my sister shaking my shoulder, tears pouring down her face. I flew up in bed, alarmed. "Ken, what is it? Are you upset about mom and me fighting?" I asked groggily. She had a fuzzy pink robe tied hastily around her, and her hair was askew under a turban printed with daisies. Her normally gentle eyes were wide with fear.

"Da-daddy," Kennedy sobbed. The clock said 5:12 am.

Panic squeezed my chest like a vise as I rubbed the sleep from my eyes. Why was she crying? "What happened?"

"He's missing," she said, wiping at her cheeks. "Uncle Ben got in touch with Mama. She's looking for him." Kennedy meant that my mom was using her red orb to search for my father. Their connection was deep and tangible; if anyone could find him when he was missing it would be her.

I shoved the covers off of myself and wrapped my arms around my sister's bony shoulders, wishing I could protect her from all the pain she felt. She was cold and shaking. "We'll find him, Ken," I promised her solemnly. "Let me get dressed. I'll be right out."

She squeezed me tightly and nodded, leaving my room and shutting the door quietly behind her. Shocked, I sat back on my bed with a huff. My dad was one of the most powerful warlocks I had ever known. The idea that he could be missing somewhere- that something could have happened to him- was just unimaginable. Cold fear wrapped around the back of my neck as I changed into black jeans, a loose white tank top, and some silver bangles. My burnt orange pendant rested against my chest like always. As an afterthought, I added the orange studs that my dad had given me for my last birthday to my ears. I quickly combed through my afro, not even caring if it looked messy.

When I got out to the living room, the air was tense and desperate. The kitchen light was on and candles made the living area glow. My mother was draped over the arm of the couch, gazing into her deep red orb beseechingly. Her braids were twisted into a knot and she wore sweatpants. "Cameron?" she called, over and over. Her eyes were far away, flicking back and forth across the orb levitating over her hand, scanning the scenes that flashed through it. The skin across her cheekbones was tight and her eyebrows were furrowed. "Cameron, it's Jada," she said loudly. "Where are you?"

Kennedy sat in a chair with her arms wrapped around her knees, watching our mother. She looked up at me as I entered the room. My mother's familiar, an orange cat named Cleo, sprawled across the back of the couch watching her seriously. They sensed our emotions easily, as our bonds were quite strong. Cleo bonded with my mother days after she was born, and has been with her ever since. Familiars live differently from other cats.

"Any luck?" I whispered to my sister, already knowing the answer.

Kennedy shook her head, dark brown eyes flashing with pain. She had changed into an aquamarine short-sleeved, v-neck shirt and black ankle jeans, with her golden pendant back around her neck. Fuzzy socks came up past her thin ankles.

My mother came out of her reverie suddenly. "Come here, girls. We are stronger together." All earlier tension forgotten, my sister and I went to sit beside her without hesitation. We clasped hands and shut our eyes, focusing.

My burnt orange orb flared up in front of my closed eyelids, joining with my mother's red and my sister's bright yellow colors. Together, they glowed and pulsed like a strong sun. When I opened my eyes, images flashed across the orbs; our Uncle Ben scouring a tree line; our Aunt Tara speaking to someone in the dark; and a flickering view of the ocean. But my father was nowhere to be seen.

"Your Uncle Ben told me that your father was supposed to show up to his house after a meeting. He was last seen suddenly heading away from camp at eight-thirty. He never reappeared," my mother murmured, watching the same images spin before us.

Minutes passed, and nothing new appeared in the huge, pulsating orbs. With a sad sigh, she released our hands. I stared at the floor in frustration. Was he hiding? Could he be hurt? Or, worse? It would take intense magic to hide from our orbs. My father had always been a strong, resolute presence in my life. When I was young and scared of the dark, he would sit by my bed until I fell asleep, telling me the old stories of our coven. He would pick me up and hug me when I was sad. He always put our family first. I couldn't let myself imagine anything happening to him.

I shook my head, fending off the negative thoughts; my dad needed me. I glanced out the large living room window into the dawn. A gray haze had settled over our village and all of the other cabins were still dark. Staring into the fog made the morning seem that much more mysterious and sinister. I made up my mind as Dezi traipsed sleepily into the room and curled up in a ball near my feet. "We need to go to Florida," I said urgently. A sleepy fire flickered in the hearth.

"Yeah," Kennedy nodded. "We'll find him there."

"No!" My mother exclaimed. "It is too dangerous! We don't know what kind of dark forces are at work here. They are obviously strong. Your father is a powerful warlock. It would take intense power to…"

I swallowed as my throat constricted. "Mama, he needs us."

"No," she said, firmly this time. "I forbid it. There are plenty of powerful witches and warlocks there already looking for him, including another Grand Warlock. All we can do is watch for him." She snapped her fingers and the red circle reappeared.

I sat silently for a few minutes, warring with myself as I glanced out the window again. I wouldn't abandon my dad. Then I looked at Kennedy and narrowed my eyes. "I'm going to…my room." I said. "I'll keep watching."

Ken stared at me numbly for a moment before getting up. "Me too. Love you, Mama."

My mother nodded absently at us, scouring deep inside her orb. Her forehead was wrinkled and the greys in her braids seemed more prominent. "I love you too, my girls."

Kennedy and I padded off towards her room. Her familiar, a black and white cat named Damon, trailed in after us. As soon as the door was shut, she turned to me, eyes wide. "We're going anyway, aren't we? Stasia?"

"We have to. Dad *needs* us," I whispered urgently, reaching for her hand. "Mom's always so worried about danger. We can't stop living just because things get dangerous. We *have* to help Dad."

"Are we going alone?" Kennedy asked quietly as she pulled on short, gray booties.

I glanced around her room, thinking. Black posters of the Eiffel Tower, Statue of Liberty, and Golden Gate Bridge set against old newspapers adorned the white walls that contrasted with her black curtains and bedspread. Books cluttered the desk and floor, and her windowsill held a pink pot with a flower from Sruthi. "No... I think we bring back-up." Snapping my fingers, I reached out to Eva again.

It took her a second to wake up. When she did, she was understandably grumpy. "Do you have any idea what time it is?" she asked groggily, pushing brown hair out of her face. Her room was dark.

"Eves, it's an emergency. My dad is missing in Florida," I whispered urgently, before she could roll over and fall back asleep.

She shot up as if she'd been stung. "What! Oh! Stasia, what happened?" She rubbed the sleep from her eyes.

"We don't know yet," Kennedy piped up, pulling her fingers through her unkempt curls and tying them up in a knot on top of her head. She pulled a baby blue bandana on next, to keep the strays out of her face. Her cheekbones and strong jawline were sharp against her skin.

"We have to go help him," I said calmly. "Will you come?" Outside, crickets were still chirping. In the distance I heard an owl hoot.

"Of course," Eva said without pause. "Let me get dressed. I'll meet you in front of your house in ten."

"Okay, but we're *kinda sorta* sneaking out," Kennedy muttered, grimacing, holding her hands behind her back.

I tried to smile, "So just be quiet and we'll come find you outside."

"I figured as much," Eva raised her thick eyebrows, peering at us through squinty eyes. With a flick of her fingers, she turned her light on and got out of bed. "See you soon," she whispered. Her violet orb went out and she disappeared from view.

"Get Sruthi," I said to Kennedy. Out of our friends, Kennedy was closest to Sruthi. Sruthi had a very laid-back, calming energy, which matched well with Kennedy's peace-making, *hakuna matata* attitude. My sister opened the door and peered out into the hallway, before giving me the 'all clear' sign. I watched her stare hard into her yellow orb. Within seconds, Sruthi appeared in view out of a deep green light.

"Hello, ladies," she murmured in a sing-song voice, as if a five a.m. wakeup call was a regular occurrence. Her lights were on and she was watering a small potted plant in her cream and lilac bedroom. Gossamer curtains hung over her window, and a white tapestry with an ornately decorated elephant rested on her wall.

"Sruth, I wouldn't call this early if it wasn't urgent-" Ken started to say, her cheeks pink.

"You ladies can call me anytime," she responded kindly, plucking at a wilting leaf.

"Thanks. But listen. My dad's in trouble in Florida. He needs our help. I called Eva already and she's coming with us. Can you?" I butted in.

Her dreamy eyes widened a fraction, but she remained calm. "Oh, sure. I'll leave my mom a note. She won't mind," she lilted. Sruthi was a bit of a hippie and dreamer, but thinking her mom wouldn't mind if she took off to Florida for a bit with friends seemed like a stretch even for her.

"Okay…if you're sure. Can you meet at my house in ten?" Kennedy asked hopefully.

She looked around her room, "Yes, I'll do that. I just have a few more plants to water," she added serenely. She started braiding her thick, dark hair back, and tied it with a white ribbon.

"Okay, time is of the essence though…" I hinted, eyeing all of the plants in her room and wondering how many "just a few" constituted.

"See you shortly," Sruthi smiled, unfazed. Her green orb disappeared.

I turned to Kennedy as she asked, "You sure about this?" Her big eyes were doubtful. I knew she was afraid.

"Positive." I hugged my sister again. "Let's leave Mom a note."

We didn't bother packing. One convenience of being witches was our ability to shape shift objects, like clothing. Eva was especially good at it. If Florida was really hot, she would have no problem turning my white tank top and jeans into a light dress. We ducked into my room and I swiped on some dark red matte lipstick and mascara.

"Why are you putting makeup on?" Ken asked impatiently.

"When you look good," I muttered, smearing highlighter along cheekbones as sharp as daggers, "you feel good. And when you feel good," I turned to my sister and stared into her wide eyes, "you kill any potential shithead warlocks that messed with your dad." Then I drew on winged eyeliner. Long eyelashes blinked back at me. I always felt most confident when I looked put together.

Kennedy muttered something under her breath about getting all boo'd up for nothing and kissed Damon goodbye, because he was far too lazy to follow us. I knew Dezi would certainly try, since she was curious and always pushed all of her limits. Kennedy had watched my mom walk to her bedroom, gazing into her orb again, while I was getting ready. So, we snuck quietly to the entryway and grabbed our cloaks and witches' hats, tugging them on. My cape was a rich burgundy, while Kennedy's was a pretty, light silver. I pulled on my over-the-knee black boots and we snuck quietly out the front door. Kennedy pointed at it and we heard the lock click shut quietly.

Hopefully, my mom wouldn't notice we were missing until we had already found our dad. Dezi had mischievously trailed us outside, acting like she wasn't interested in seeing where I was going. She wandered over to a tree and started scratching it, but I could see her shooting glances my way.

The early morning air was crisp and the sky was still a light gray. I was grateful for my warm cloak. Eva was standing beside a tree in our side yard, scanning a map of the Florida Keys that I assumed she'd shape shifted from a different piece of paper. Under her white cape was a lilac shirt tucked into denim overalls, and a pair of scuffed up white sneakers kicked at the ground. Her short hair was pushed behind her ears and poked out from under her witch's hat.

"Hey," Eva whispered. "I know where the coven is. I guess that's where we start, right?" Responsible and composed, she was usually the leader of our little girl gang. Behind her glasses, dark, smoky eye-liner and long lashes rimmed her light hazel eyes, which were focused on the paper in her hands. She always used logic as a defense from panic. Magenta lipstick lined her thick lips and the violet gems in her witch's hat sparkled in the morning light. Like me, Eva always liked to look put together, even if she didn't feel it.

Kennedy nodded her approval. "That sounds like a good start to me. I can't believe this is happening." She pulled chapstick out of her pocket and spread it across her lips nervously. I noticed her hand was trembling.

I reached out and touched her arm.

"We'll find him," Eva promised. A cold breeze rippled through the air, playing with our hair, and making the hairs on my arms stand up. Cold air had a way of bringing you to your knees and reminding you that you were alive.

Finally, Sruthi showed up. She was wearing her typical *shalwar kameez*; a long, pink and teal tunic, tights, and black flats. She had a pink flower pin on her mint cape, and little daffodil earring studs. It was obvious the girl had an affinity for plants. "Sorry I'm late," she murmured, her breath showing in a cloud of mist. "One of my cacti is having a tough recovery." Her witch's hat was slightly crumpled.

"Sruth," Kennedy said, "We really appreciate you coming."

"But like, priorities," Eva chimed in, a smirk playing at her lips.

Sruthi blushed, but a small smile stayed on her face.

"Ready?" I asked. They all nodded, looking slightly queasy.

"We're four strong, capable women. We've got this," Sruthi said bravely, nudging my sister with her elbow.

"The girl gang," Kennedy agreed with a hesitant smile.

"Coven version," I smiled.

Eva nodded and adjusted her tortoise shell glasses, "Let's go save your dad."

We all clasped hands. Slowly, our palms lit up. Orange joined yellow, violet, and green against the dawn. As the energy grew bigger, I squeezed Sruthi and Kennedy's hands tighter, and saw Eva do the same across from me. In seconds, we vanished into a burst of white light with a small swishing sound.

4

Hot and Bold

In what felt like seconds, my boots landed lightly on thick white sand. I spun around and released the girls' hands, taking in my surroundings. We were on a deserted beach. Palm trees stood tall and swayed, their shadows dancing across the ground. Blinding sunshine came from almost directly overhead because of the time difference, and it bounced like diamonds over clear blue water to our right. The air was stiflingly hot and dense, but felt electric too.

"It could be worse," Eva grinned, spinning in a circle. Her white cape and brown hair fluttered in a steamy breeze. The map hung down at her side.

Sruthi bent down to the ground and placed her palms flat against the hot sand. Her cape billowed out and wrapped around her as she closed her eyes and hummed, her long lashes resting against sharp cheekbones. The waves lapped at the shoreline behind us.

"Can you feel anything?" I asked, figuring that she was using her connection to the earth to sense people nearby. She picked up and held small rocks in her hand.

Eva held up the piece of paper. "I can just check..."

"The camp is not far off. The palm trees say so," Sruthi said softly, opening her hazel eyes. "To the north."

"...the map." Eva finished, lips drawn in a tight line.

Kennedy smiled and grabbed my hand. "We're almost there! We're going to save Dad!"

"Hang on a second," Eva said, closing her eyes. She clapped her hands and her cape made a whistling sound before growing thinner and thinner, until the material looked like silk. "Anyone else?" she asked cockily, one eyebrow raised.

"Yeah, it's like 900 degrees," Kennedy agreed.

I laughed and nodded, feeling weightless now that we were here.

"Me too," Sruthi piped up.

The wool turned to silk against my back, and instantly I felt cooler. Looking around at the other girls, I realized my skin still felt like it was prickling from an electric current.

"Can you feel that?" It looked like the air was shimmering around us. My palms felt like they were touching static.

Kennedy nodded.

"It's because we're so close to the equator," Eva said, adjusting her tortoise-shell glasses and taking on the tone of a professor. "The Florida Keys have held deep magic for millennia. Basically, it comes down to-"

I cleared my throat, raising an eyebrow.

"Right, okay, let's go," she mumbled, looking at the ground. "I'll tell you later."

We followed Sruthi, who was being guided by the palm leaves or something, away from the shoreline and towards a dense jungle of plants. Kennedy walked behind her, and I made up the end of the line. Our jeweled witches' hats kept the bright sun out of our eyes. We traipsed through ferns, slim branches, and mossy tree trunks as the sun beat down on us.

"Are you sure we're going the right way?" Kennedy asked nervously, her hands in her jean pockets.

Sruthi smiled kindly at her, "I'm positive. We're not far." She reached out to touch Kennedy's arm reassuringly and Ken blushed. Sruthi's long, dark hair came loose of its ribbon and pulsed around her as she tapped into the earth, fingers gliding from tree trunk to trunk.

Eva kept checking the map, her lips turned downwards.

All I could think about was my dad. I wondered what had happened in those few short hours since I had glimpsed him in my orb to make him unfindable. What could he be hiding from?

I watched Kennedy repeatedly swat at the same mosquito, until Eva finally pointed at it and zapped it.

"Oh yeah," Ken mumbled to herself.

Mere minutes later, we stumbled out of the trees and into the coven's camp. Unlike our warm, sturdy wood cabins, their homes were made of tiki wood, clay, and palm fronds. They were a smaller coven, with only sixteen individual homes. I remembered my dad telling me that they had branched off from another local coven a few years before, and were still growing.

Immediately, I saw a familiar face. Uncle Ben walked purposefully from a hut near us, only to freeze in his path when he saw us. His eyes flitted from face to face. "Anastasia? Kennedy? What-"

I stepped forward and stubbornly stuck my chin out. "We had to come help," I told him, more confidently than I felt. Carrying myself tall and speaking loudly had always made me seem like I knew what I was doing in the past. I knew my dad was somewhere nearby, and he needed us; I could feel it in my bones now that we were here. And I would help him slay whatever dragons stood in the way of him coming home.

Okay, well, dragons aren't real. But that's not the point.

"Yeah, Dad needs us," Kennedy said, mimicking my posture.

"At your service," Eva smiled.

To my surprise, my dad's younger brother didn't put up a fight. "Great, we need all the hands we can get." Uncle Ben was tall and muscular, with a shaved head and dark, tired eyes. He wore thin silver and royal purple robes. He stood confidently, and commanded the area around him. "Come this way. We'll go see what your Auntie needs." He didn't wait to be introduced to our friends, but strode off to our left.

Nodding, I led the way after him. He didn't head back into his hut, but around a corner to an unlit fire pit. My Aunt Tara sat cross legged, eyes shut, humming softly to herself. She wore a ruby shirt and gray slacks under her ash cloak. A witch's hat was perched on her head. She had the darkest skin of any witch I had ever known, and was by far the most beautiful, with long, wavy tresses of deep black hair. Her palms vibrated slightly in her lap against her muscled thighs. Her thick lips were puckered as she concentrated. The air around her seemed absolutely still. Even the shrill birds had stopped cawing to each other.

"Tara," my uncle murmured softly, and her chocolate eyes shot open. But she didn't look as surprised to see us as Uncle Ben had been.

"Good, I just saw you arrive," she said musically, standing up gracefully. A dancer, Aunt Tara was lithe and delicate. She was also really gifted at seeing the present in her mind if she focused really hard, a talent that many witches and warlocks struggled to achieve. She walked over and hugged each of us. "I'm so sorry about this. We'll find him," my aunt vowed. "I've been looking for him all day." Her voice was serious but calm. "We've moved all around the camp to see if I can pick him up anywhere. So far, no luck."

I saw Uncle Ben shoot her a look over Kennedy's head.

I squeezed her back, taking comfort in her embrace. Aunt Tara was one of my favorite people in the world, and I completely understood why my uncle had moved so far to marry her and join her coven. Even if that coven lived in unbearable humidity. She was so smart and sweet and graceful, and always put others first.

I introduced my friends, and then looked at my uncle. "Where do we start?"

He quickly relayed a more detailed version of the story my mom had told us. The Grand Warlock of Aunt Tara's coven died of mysterious causes a few days before. He had disappeared for two days, before showing up dead at the nearest river, which he never visited. Immediately, my uncle started looking into it, and things didn't add up.

First of all, the Grand Warlock was not supposed to be anywhere near the river on that day; he was scheduled to lead a council that night and usually spent the days working on strengthening and increasing the size of their government from his office.

Second, my uncle said, he had left a fire burning near his hut right before he went missing. It seemed like he had been planning to come back. The Grand Warlock was a careful, responsible man, and he had not previously left a fire unsupervised. But that didn't worry my uncle as much as the next part.

When two members of the coven found him on their way to go fishing, there were obvious signs of a scuffle beside his body. As a powerful warlock, there was almost no need for him to have ever used physical force to attack or defend himself; he could easily protect himself with magic. And lastly, there was no outward sign of a cause of death, meaning the most likely thing that killed him was a curse. That made the whole coven suspects, as well as anyone who could have wandered upon it.

My uncle had expressed his concerns to a select few, including the Grand Warlock's brother, Diego, who moved to Florida to take his place. Diego had promised Uncle Ben he would look into it while my Aunt Tara's sister, Denise, performed a magical autopsy. My uncle also called my father, a trusted Grand Warlock, who promptly came out to visit. He agreed with my uncle after hearing the story, and was doing his own investigation when he too disappeared. My uncle desperately wanted to find my dad before he ended up dead as well.

Anxiety clawed at my stomach while he explained; I needed to get out and start combing the area for my father. Kennedy seemed to sense my tension and reached out to hold my hand. Grateful, I squeezed her fingers.

Uncle Ben told us they had followed my dad's path around a few huts in the village, through the woods, and to the river, but the trail went cold there last night. The new Grand Warlock apparently didn't seem concerned, spending most of his time in his office and saying he was sure that my dad would come wandering back with the mystery solved. But my uncle and aunt weren't so sure. They suspected dark forces were at play.

Little kids ran past, screaming, laughing, and chasing each other, but their joy felt far away. The adults were walking around with serious expressions knitting their brows. I nervously pulled at my hair, watching my friends faces register the gravity of the situation we were in. Eva's forehead was furrowed with worry lines and her light eyes were hard. Sruthi kept cracking her knuckles and shifting her feet. Kennedy was biting her lip. We needed action to replace insecurity.

"...so, we're going to start there. Okay?" A deep voice broke through my reverie.

"Yeah," my sister said.

"Anastasia?" My uncle had concern clearly splashed across his face.

"Sorry, what?" I mumbled. I focused on his face, although it felt like his lips were moving faster than his voice.

"I said, Tara and I are heading to the waterfall near where the Grand Warlock was found. We want you girls to follow the trail around the village, talk to some people, see if you can pick up on anything. Then come meet us at the river, by the waterfall. You girls said your friend will be able to guide you to us, right?"

"Oh, um, yes, yeah, Sruthi can do that." I nodded.

She shot me a confident smile as she pulled strands of her long hair back into its braid.

"Okay, meet us in a few hours, and we will come up with a plan. Tara and I are going to take a long way and see if we can find any other paths from your dad. We'll meet you there."

After they walked off, Eva looked at us and lifted her chin. "Alright, we can do this. I think the smartest thing will be to split up and get through twice as much twice as fast. Sruth- go with Anastasia. You guys start on that half," she pointed to her right. "And Ken- you come with me. We'll start over there. Ana, use your acting skills, will you? Convince them to tell you everything they know."

I could see that Kennedy was hoping to be paired with Sruthi by the way she stared at her. I met Eva's penetrating gaze feeling like a child, but I would never let that show. Pulling myself up tall, I took a deep breath and nodded. Sruthi linked her arm through mine and we walked off. The morning sun beat down relentlessly as we knocked on doors. The first two were empty, but at the third, an old woman answered with a smile and a pile of curly, white hair atop her head.

"Hi, ma'am, we're sorry to bother you," Sruthi said sweetly, "but we could really use your help."

The woman's sea blue eyes were soft and kind as she appraised us, especially focusing on Sruthi's pretty outfit.

"I have to say, I really admire your petunias," Sruthi started to say, pointing at the ground, but I cleared my throat and cut in.

"My dad was here... and he, well, he went missing yesterday," I said tensely. "He was looking into the death of... your..."

"Our Grand Warlock, Antony," she suggested kindly. A few wispy clouds passed overhead.

"Yes," I gulped and met her eyes, focusing all of my energy on what I wanted. The truth.

"I heard the awful news," she said, stepping outside into the baking heat with a sad smile. "I'm sorry about your dad. I hope he comes back."

"Well, that's what we need your help with, ma'am," Sruthi told her, gently elbowing me in the ribs.

Holding the old woman's gaze, I said confidently, "I need to know anything you can tell us about your Warlock disappearing, or my father. It would be *really* helpful," my voice took on the persuasive lilt of the siren.

The old lady looked down at the rock-strewn ground, and I noticed that she wore Birkenstocks with her beige dress when I followed her gaze. "Of course. I wish I had something to tell you, but I don't leave my hut much."

Discouragement ran through my veins like liquid ice. "Oh. So, you didn't see him?"

She shook her head and smiled, "No, no, that's not what I meant. I did run into your father yesterday, on his way to the new Warlock's home, and he was a perfect gentleman. It's just too bad," she said to me.

"He went to the new Warlocks house?" I asked with surprise. Uncle Ben and my mom hadn't mentioned that.

Her eyes were troubled. "Why, yes, I believe he said that was where he was starting his investigation. Maybe the Warlock knows where your father was headed."

"Thank you!" I exclaimed, already running through the scorching sand.

Sruthi caught up to me easily, and pulled me to a stop. "You don't know where you're going. Hang on. Let me feel for it." Frustrated, I nodded. Sruthi was right. She closed her eyes and rested her palms against the grainy earth again. All of the tension left her face and she looked back up at me serenely. "This way."

We found Eva and Kennedy walking dejectedly away from some homes on the far perimeter. Eva was flipping a dark stone in her hand, and its form kept shifting to a pearly marble and back. Her overalls and white sneakers were dusty. Kennedy's forehead was lined with concern as she scanned the nearby trees. Her curls were getting frizzier the longer we stayed in the humidity, forcing their way out of her bun.

"Hey!" I exclaimed, my throat dry. I jogged up to them, with Sruthi steps behind me. I placed my hand on Kennedy's slim arm as I caught my breath. The sun was really bearing down on us and the breeze that made the palm trees dance earlier had worn off. Sweat beaded the back of my neck, but my hat kept it out of my eyes.

"Any word from Mom yet?" Ken asked me right away. We all started walking towards benches along the tree line.

"No. You?"

"No." Palm trees rustled around us.

"Well, I'm glad. She probably figures we're still asleep and is too distracted worrying about Dad to even think about us." I said flippantly, wiping at sweat on my forehead.

Kennedy was gnawing on her lip. "I'm just dreading getting yelled at."

I forced a smile. "You shouldn't be afraid of someone else being angry with you if it's for the right reasons. Besides, if we find Dad, she'll have no reason to be mad." I pulled her arm through mine and straightened my witch's hat.

Sruthi glanced up at the sky as she said, "An old woman told us Stasia's dad was meeting with the Grand Warlock. I think we need to go there now and see where the trail leaves off."

Eva's eyebrows knitted behind her glasses, "I don't think that's such a good idea."

"Why?" Kennedy and I exclaimed together, shocked. It seemed like the obvious next step. Sruthi reached out, resting her palm against a tree trunk and closing her eyes.

Eva pulled the piece of paper out of her pocket and tapped it lightly. A more detailed geographical map of the area appeared. Distracted, she looked up at us. "We're going to find your dad. I promise. But, let's break this down. The old Grand Warlock passes away mysteriously. Then his brother shows up to take charge. Already suspicious."

"You think it's-" Kennedy loudly started to say. I squeezed her arm.

"Let's just consider this," Eva continued. "Then someone from the outside, your dad, comes to town to solve the mystery. He *also* disappears."

"Maybe he was onto something," Sruthi murmured, dropping her hand from the tree. "And he had to be stopped. I sense malevolence here."

"So, I really don't think a good place to start is with the new Grand Warlock. Think about it. Where is he? Someone new comes to his coven and disappears, and he can't be found looking for him? He's hiding. I'm calling it," Eva said decisively.

We all grew quiet.

"I feel so useless!" Kennedy suddenly exclaimed. "I wish I could help more. Anastasia's good at convincing people to help us, Sruthi can sense things and directions from the Earth, and Eva's great at changing objects to make them more useful *and* using logic.

And I'm just, here." She pulled her hat off of her head and flattened it against her lap, lips in a pout.

"You *are* useful," Eva murmured from beside her. "You keep us all together, you keep the peace, you keep us going."

"Yeah, we need you, Ken," I added, biting my lip.

"Don't doubt that. We're the girl gang," Sruthi chimed in.

Kennedy nodded, pulling herself together with a shaky breath. "You're right. Now isn't the time to worry about me either."

"You know," Sruthi said, "if your theory is right, Eva, then their uncle is in grave danger."

"Shit."

5

The First Grand Witch

"Honestly, it's time we put women in charge of covens," Kennedy complained breathlessly as we trampled through the jungle underbrush. Sruthi looked like she could die of happiness surrounded by all the green ferns, fauna, and palms. "I mean really," Kennedy continued, "how often do you see Grand Witches? Ever?"

"Definitely agree, but what makes you say that?" Eva asked. Her brown hair was starting to get frizzier too. She had transformed a rock into a knife before we started heading to the river, and was hacking away as she led the rest of us. Sruthi kept us on track from behind her.

"Witches would never kill each other and fight like this over covens," Kennedy replied. "I think it's testosterone. We are better at mediating and not making rash decisions."

"Also, less murderers are women, statistically," I added, batting at mosquitos. Eva smirked at me.

"I'm just saying. It should at least be proportional. All this 'Grand Warlock' stuff is so outdated. I want to be the first 'Grand Witch' in our coven. I could *really* lead a coven." Ken smacked a palm out of the way. "I'm fair, straight-forward, and compassionate."

"And very modest," I grinned at her, knowing she was right.

"Yeah, you could," Eva smiled and teased, "down with the patriarchy."

"Turn right up at that bend," Sruthi pointed. "And then we'll just follow the river."

"We could have yearly meetings among covens to discuss relations- Eva, you would be in charge of that. You know so much about other covens," Kennedy added.

"It's funny that you say that. I have been thinking about becoming a diplomat."

"See! I'm onto something…"

"Because I want to travel a lot," Eva said.

"Well, you'd get to with that job. You could visit covens all over the world."

"Yeah, travel is super important to me."

I was only half-listening, letting my body follow the other three. The other part of my brain was thinking about my dad, wondering what had happened to him. He'd always been a good listener and an even better compromiser; Kennedy had gotten her peace-making attitude from him. I just couldn't imagine him fighting anyone. He was a strong warlock, there was no doubt, but I didn't think he'd ever had to use his powers in a serious battle. It made me worry about how prepared he could have been. Memories of him teaching us how to levitate pebbles without touching them, laughing and picking up Kennedy in his strong arms whenever she grew frustrated, and being endlessly patient as we learned new spells and tricks spun around my head. I knew I had to find him. I had to save him.

We got to the river and they paused.

"Stasia, you okay?" Sruthi asked me gently. The water lapped at the bank behind her, fighting the current to make it back to the shore restlessly.

I shook my head and came back to reality, forcing a smile. "Yeah, I'm just worried about my dad. I can't believe my biggest stressor last night was going off to acting school, and now this…"

She reached out and touched my arm. Her hazel eyes were gentle as she lilted, "We're going to find him. I promise. It's why we're here… we've got powers, and we can do this."

"Yeah, four badass ladies to the rescue!" Kennedy cheered, clapping. I grinned at her, glad to see her coming out of her funk.

"And then you'll get into acting school," Sruthi promised, her accent reassuring. "Far, far away."

Kennedy's face suddenly puckered as she brushed stray curls out of her eyes.

"Maybe," I murmured.

Eva groaned. "Okay, not to ruin the moment, but I'm starving."

"You literally ruin every moment by saying you're hungry," Ken teased, putting a hand on her hip.

I realized that we hadn't eaten anything since the night before. I looked around as if a cauldron would just appear in the middle of the forest.

Kennedy wiggled her fingers at Eva with a mischievous grin, "What are ya whipping up for us, Chef?" We all knew Eva was the superior one at transfiguration.

Eva rolled her eyes and put her hand on her hip. "I need something to transform, don't I? Sruth?"

Sruthi beamed and started plucking wilting leaves off of a nearby tree. Kennedy got up to help her.

"This never gets old," I murmured. Anxiety still filled my stomach, but my friends gave off such positive, hopeful energy that I couldn't resist feeling lighter.

"Any requests?"

"I'll take a granola bar," I said. "Throw in some fruit, too."

"*Ohhh*, sounds good," Sruthi added, handing her the assortment of leaves. "I'll have the same."

Kennedy asked for avocado toast, eggs, some juice, and a banana, and Eva looked ready to punch her. Laughing, Kennedy held her hands up in the air in surrender as Eva's started to glow violet around the leaves.

We sat around in a circle by the river, stuffing our faces full of fruit and granola. Our hats rested at our sides and our cloaks were spread out behind us. Birds chirped all around the river and little lizards darted from tree to tree. The jungle was peaceful and warm until Kennedy reminded us that alligators lived here. Eva and I scooted away from the river without a second thought as Kennedy laughed, but Sruthi remained serenely by the edge, saying, "I will sense any animal that comes near, and the alligators mean no harm if we leave them alone."

"Till they're hungry," Eva joked darkly. Every little crack in the underbrush suddenly seemed sinister.

"Hmm, pretty sure they'd harm you even if they weren't," Kennedy added, bursting into giggles. Sruthi grinned at her.

The sun filtered down through the canopy and turned everything around us golden. Sruthi re-braided her hair for the millionth time.

"Maybe you should become a hair stylist, with how often you have to play with yours," Eva teased.

"Yeah MaryAnn's not all that great," Kennedy complained, talking about the only stylist in our coven.

"At least not with black hair," I sniffed.

Sruthi patted her hairs into place and grinned. "No, I really do think I'm going to work in film, and specialize in environmentalism. I'll find a way to get around the coven's rules. I could focus on documentaries and help all the plants grow happily."

"So that I can eat them," Kennedy snorted.

Sruthi glowered. "I've always wanted to work in film. Anastasia and I have been shooting those little movies for so long. And you know I love to get my hands dirty. I think we need more voices advocating for environmental preservation and using renewable resources."

I nodded fervently.

While chewing, Eva said, "well, *I'm* still going into government. International relations or something, like she said, where I get to travel a lot."

"We know," Kennedy smirked. "You've only said it 900 times."

Eva snapped her fingers and acorns rained down on Kennedy's head, causing them both to burst out laughing.

"Yeah, you'd be great at that," I told her, a smile tugging at my lips. "Relations really seem to be your thing." I pointed back and forth between her and Kennedy.

"What about you, Ken?" Sruthi asked when the hail storm ended. The last time my sister and I had talked about it, Ken had told me she wanted to be a magical vet and work with familiars.

"I think I'm moving towards the idea of working in government too. Eventually becoming the next Grand Witch. I was being serious."

"Yes, girl!" Sruthi said excitedly. Her face was lit by the sunshine and two little weeds had started tilting towards her while we'd been eating.

"Yeah, I'm tired of feeling underrepresented. Besides, I've toyed with the idea that covens shouldn't have to hide anymore." She shook her head sadly, "I know what everyone will say. That it's too dangerous. That they don't understand us. That they are afraid of us and they want us gone. That we can't repeat history. Well, I want to change that."

The mood perceptively darkened.

Eva nodded grimly. "I think we all do."

"We could even use our powers to better the environment," Sruthi suggested. My sister smiled at her.

"The first black Grand Witch, coming through!" I crowed. "With big changes on the way."

We sat quietly for a moment, smiling at each other and imagining a world where we didn't have to hide our powers, but could use them for good.

"And we know you want to be an actress," Eva said to me, breaking the silence. "Our little drama queen."

I pursed my lips but laughed. "Yeah. I want to tell people of colors' stories. Good stories. Brave stories. With strong characters. I want to star in movies, and show little girls everywhere that we can do it *too*. That we can be badass characters like superheroes and doctors and presidents. That we can be the lead role and *still* have the movies make tons of money. And beyond that, I want to show *witches* that we can do it."

"That would be nice for a change," Eva said, holding my gaze.

"I just feel incredibly limited and... powerless here. In the coven. I mean, we're practically invisible. And being an actor gives you a voice and a platform where you can tell stories and bring about change. You know?"

"Yes, sis!" Kennedy cheered. "I can't wait."

"Maybe I'll play you in a movie," I said softly. "The *first* Grand Witch."

"I'll be at the premiere," Eva said sweetly.

"So will I!" Sruthi chimed in. "Someone's got to get an award for directing it."

We all grinned.

Two birds soared overhead as we finished eating.

Then Eva got back down to business with a sigh. "So, we're going to meet with your uncle and aunt, see what they've found, and go from there. Your dad was supposed to meet with the Grand Warlock, he was last seen coming into the woods, and his trail left off along this river. He can't be far."

"Should we just yell for him?" I asked, brushing crumbs off of my lap and flexing my arms.

Kennedy frowned as Eva said, "I don't think that's such a good idea. We don't know who, or what, else could be out here."

We all grimaced, looking into the dense, green maze around us.

"Just up there," Sruthi murmured, holding her mint cloak out of the way as she cut between two slim trees. "I can sense them up ahead." We followed her tensely, unsure of what we would find ahead.

To my equal relief and disappointment, my aunt and uncle were alone.

"Anastasia! Kennedy!" Uncle Benjamin called. "Glad you made it." Aunt Tara was sitting on the river bank cross-legged again. Her eyes were closed and she looked peaceful as she searched around us with her gift.

"Any luck so far?" I asked hopefully, my voice trembling. I felt Kennedy come stand beside me.

I saw something hard pass over my uncle's eyes, and then he said, "Not yet. But Tara thinks she might feel him nearby. So... I'm letting her do her thing." He ran his hand over his close-shaven head. Without a word, Sruthi went to sit by Aunt Tara and rested her palms against the ground. Kennedy stared after her, re-adjusting her bandana.

"Uncle Ben," I said, "tell us about your new Grand Warlock." Eva's eyes were tight behind her tortoise-shell glasses and she jutted her chin out. Kennedy started pacing.

He met my eyes, and I saw it there. He was questioning it too. "Our last Grand Warlock, Antony, came to Florida almost twenty years ago from Puerto Rico. Antony was elected to be the Grand Warlock here a few years after that, when the one before him passed. There was no competition; everyone liked Antony. And Antony did a great job of leading us since then. He left behind his brother Diego and his father, who was a Grand Warlock over in Puerto Rico. When his father grew sick and was too weak to leave the house, Diego took over governing that coven and caring for his father. And then he came here," he said bitterly.

"When did his brother come?" Eva asked quietly. Palm fronds swayed behind us as another hot breeze rippled through the air.

"Diego got here a day after Antony went missing. Someone notified him. He seems nice enough, just quiet, keeps to himself for the most part. Doesn't seem especially focused on figuring out what happened to his brother, although he *has* been gone all day looking for your dad."

"We think it might be him," I said quietly, looking around. My heart was hammering in my chest. Eva nodded.

Uncle Ben's face darkened. "I'm starting to have the same thoughts, Anastasia."

"But why?" Kennedy asked. "Why hurt two Grand Warlocks?"

It was Eva who answered her. "Think about it, Ken. With the first one, he gets promoted to Grand Warlock here. Then, if he gets rid of your dad, he protects his secret."

"We need to find him," I said. The river churned beside us.

"I'll kill Diego if he hurts my dad," Kennedy growled. My eyes narrowed and my hands were fists at my sides.

Uncle Ben held his hands up quickly. "Hopefully it won't come to that."

Eva's eyes were sad but her shoulders were set. "I'll do whatever it takes to help you. I promise." Her white cloak billowed out behind her.

Aunt Tara stood up lithely and walked towards us. Quietly, she said, "This is near where Antony was found. I thought it would help me to sit here and search. And I think it has. I still cannot see anything, but I feel myself being tugged north. We should go." She looked firmly at Uncle Ben.

He sighed and looked around the jungle growth before saying, "They'll just follow us if we leave them here."

A small smile tugged at the corner of her lips. "Let's go, ladies."

<u>6</u>
Defiance

We were cutting through dense underbrush when my orb lit up in front of my face. Dread filled my stomach because I knew it was going to be my mom. Sure enough, her outraged face appeared inside a red circle seconds later. We all slowed to a stop.

"What the *hell* were you two thinking?" she demanded. Her skin was tight across her cheekbones as she pushed her braids out of her face. "A note? A *note*? Are you kidding me? Get back here right *now*! With all this stress over your father, you two thought it was a good idea if you *also* went missing?!"

I took a deep breath. "Mama, we can't do that. Dad needs us."

"Please don't be mad, Mom," Kennedy said, hating tension.

"There are plenty of people looking for your father!" her deep voice shook, enunciating each word. "I need you two girls safe at home, where I can protect you!"

I calmly explained, "We're with Uncle Ben and Aunt Tara. We are safe. We think we're onto something."

"I can feel it in my gut that there is danger," she replied tersely, shaking out her hands.

To my surprise, Kennedy suddenly puffed out her chest and said firmly, "We're staying, Mom. We're going to bring Dad home."

"Jada, we will not let anything happen to your daughters," Aunt Tara promised, holding her hand over her heart.

My mother was silent for a moment, staring off into space.

I took advantage of the quiet and said pleadingly, "Mom, I understand that you're afraid of the outside world. I really do. I know you're scared. But you can't stop us from living. You shouldn't stop us from trying to find Dad. You have to trust that we can take care of ourselves already. We learned from you. We are strong witches."

Her lips trembled and she nodded. "I'm coming. I'll pack a bag and meet you within the hour."

With Sruthi and Aunt Tara leading the way, we arrived atop a tall, jagged cliff overlooking a canyon in what felt like minutes. It didn't look anything like the Floridian landscape we'd been trekking through all day. I could feel the tension vibrating off of Aunt Tara, and knew we had to be close. We picked our way over rocks and through shrubs towards the edge. The river ran along the right side of the cliff and cascaded down to the basin in a loud waterfall. "That is where I feel myself being pulled," Aunt Tara pointed to the top of it.

The field below us was enclosed on all sides by walls of rock, and was full of wildflowers and green weeds. The sun cascaded across the valley from the west. It would be a peaceful place to visit under different circumstances. We were all standing there silently, taking it in, when Eva pointed to the right and exclaimed, "Over there! Look!"

A hundred yards below us was a small hut, almost tucked away into the rock wall near the pounding water. The door flap was waving in the breeze but no sound omitted from it.

"I haven't seen that before," Aunt Tara said, eyebrows drawing together.

Sruthi got down on the ground and placed her hands against a large rock. She closed her eyes, and her pink and teal *shalwar kameez* rustled in the hot breeze. Her long braid hung down her back, and she tilted her face up to the sun, which danced across her straight nose and arched lips. "I sense people. Below."

We all tensed.

Uncle Ben and Aunt Tara crept to the very edge of the precipice, motioning for us to stay back. The birds were quiet and the air seemed to grow still as we watched them make their way closer to the steep incline. They ducked down, heads close together, watching. All eyes focused on the hut below but no one said a word.

I stood protectively in front of Ken, my hands trembling and glowing a rusty orange at my sides. My cape and witch's hat should have kept me cool beneath the shadow of the palms, but I could feel sweat sliding down my neck. I glanced over at Uncle Ben. He started to nod to us when Aunt Tara gasped, her face shaded by a wispy cloud. Her eyes were closed but her mouth hung open in shock. Her thick lips pulled back over her teeth as she whispered vehemently, "He's here."

Uncle Ben took her hand in his, "Who, Tara? Diego?"

"Yes," she hissed. "And their father." Her dark eyes opened and shot to us, and there was fear clearly drawn across them. "He's still alive," she whispered. "But barely." Her long, wavy hair hung around her elbows.

Uncle Ben turned to the four of us and held his hands up. "Stay here," he commanded, dark eyes flashing.

"No-" Kennedy and I started to exclaim at the same time, but he cut us off.

"Your Aunt Tara and I are far more experienced. Let us go scout it out. I can't have you risking your lives." Stress pulled at his forehead.

As I opened my mouth to argue, Aunt Tara said, "Your mother will be here any minute and she will need you. We promised to keep you safe. We will fly down and check it out."

I heard Kennedy's mouth shut hard. Uncle Ben stared into my eyes and I finally nodded. Sruthi and Eva shared exasperated looks but said nothing. My uncle's face was determined.

Uncle Ben placed a hand on Aunt Tara's arm and they walked to the edge. With one last glance back at us, they jumped off. Aunt Tara rested her palms by her sides and they glided down to the ground gracefully, capes billowing out behind them. Sruthi leaned against a particularly thick gray rock. The air around us was as silent as death.

I crept to the very edge of the cliff and knelt down, leaning forward, ready to lunge across the opening at a moment's notice. I kept one hand up in front of Kennedy to stop her from following me. I could never live with myself if something happened to my dad *and* her. But she took my hand and twined her fingers through mine.

Eva was looking back and forth from one edge of the valley to the other, and I could see her measuring the distance. Cut like a deep bowl, it was about a football field in length and width, with at least a forty foot drop down. She met Sruthi's eyes. "We need to get to the other side. Strategically, it makes our chances better."

Sruthi nodded and pulled her witch's hat down harder over her ears. Her braid hung down her back, but little wisps of hair circled her kind face. She stuck a hand out, which Eva grasped.

"Are you sure..." Kennedy glanced beseechingly at them, and it was clear that she was terrified that they would get hurt, but their faces were calm and determined.

Eva smiled at my sister. "We need to have the best vantage points to protect your aunt and uncle."

"It's best to have eyes from all angles," Sruthi agreed.

I looked at both of them and nodded solemnly.

"Girl gang," Sruthi whispered with a smile.

"Always," I said. Ken nodded fervently at my side.

"Love you," Eva said softly, holding my eyes.

Their palms began to glow green and violet, and then they disappeared.

7

Girl Power

I could breathe again when my best friends reappeared on the other side of the canyon. They knelt down and watched my aunt and uncle cut across the field below us. I was concentrating hard, ready to shoot off spells, when the door flap of the hut suddenly pushed open.

My uncle and aunt froze where they were, staring in disbelief. Aunt Tara cleared her throat and her voice boomed confidently. "What's going on, Diego? We're looking for Cameron. Have you seen him?" Her chin jutted towards the sky, pointing her witch's hat at the sun, but I noticed that her fingers twitched at her sides, ready to produce a spell.

Diego took a few steps away from the hut, meandering closer to them, and I watched his eyes slide down to her long fingers. He had dark black hair and mean, squinting amber eyes. His burgundy cloak hugged his muscular arms, which he held in front of himself as if warding off an attack. He didn't speak.

"Diego," Uncle Ben thundered, stepping through the dying grass. "Where is my brother? What is going on?"

Aunt Tara seethed, flinging her gray cloak out behind her. "I know he's here. I can sense him."

An ominous smile flitted across Diego's face as he stood his ground. His thick brows furrowed, but most of his face was shaded by his hat. "You must be mistaken," he said amicably, but something sinister boiled beneath the surface. Black boots poked out beneath his cape.

I snapped my fingers as quietly as possible and my orb leapt up from my palm. I saw Kennedy and my friends do the same moments after. Eva held both hands in front of her chest.

"Where is my brother?" Uncle Ben yelled again. The muscles in his arm flexed, and his hands glowed a faint purple. Aunt Tara leaned forward and pulled her arms behind herself, ready to shoot a spell at him.

"I wouldn't," Diego murmured dangerously, holding up a finger. The waterfall roared just to his right. "If you value your lives at all, you won't put up a fight." A light burgundy haze started to outline his body. "If you do, the same fate that met your brother will happen to you."

With a snarl, Uncle Ben shot a plum lightning strike at Diego, who quickly deflected it with a shield spell. Diego held up a hand to stop them and snapped his fingers. The hut flap ruffled again, and my father drifted out lazily. He floated along rigidly in a red cloud, and his skin looked sallow. His eyes were shut and he didn't move. Spray from the waterfall rained down around him.

I heard Kennedy gasp beside me, and my knees grew weak. I clutched the ground in front of me to keep myself upright, and felt warmth and energy course into my hand. Sruth. I straightened my spine as anger rushed up it.

"Wait," Ken murmured. I saw that she was digging her nails into her palms.

Frustrated, I didn't move and watched helplessly. I had to drag my eyes from my father, who looked so lifeless, to the scene unwinding before me. The sun was sinking below the tops of the palm trees, and it cast a golden glow across the field.

Uncle Ben looked shocked, but Aunt Tara's eyes were slits.

Eva appeared in my orb. "Your father's in a trance," she whispered. "It looks like old, dark magic. Diego must be trying to steal his powers."

"We have to stop him," Kennedy growled. Sruthi met her gaze from across the canyon and I felt my sister take a shaky breath. I gripped her hand tightly.

I watched my uncle Ben send more purple flashes Diego's way as he approached, but they all ricocheted off of an invisible shield. Aunt Tara pulled her hands behind her head again and then threw them forward, sending icy gray spells at Diego that hit him like sleet. They fizzled and popped around him, but he remained unscathed, a small smirk on his face.

"Soon his powers will be mine, and there's nothing you can do," Diego boasted, zapping Uncle Ben with a red curse. He fell to his knees, and when he stood back up, he was clutching his ribs.

"Is that what you did to Antony?" Uncle Ben demanded breathlessly. One of his spells sliced the top off of a palm tree and it crashed loudly to the ground.

"I will take all the power I need to become the strongest warlock this world has ever seen!" Diego bellowed, sending a cloud the color of blood flying at my uncle. Before Uncle Ben could move it enveloped him, and he froze just like my father.

"No!" Shrieked Aunt Tara. Again, she pulled her arms above her head, and the gray that circled around her looked like a tornado. With all of her strength she shot it towards Diego. He stumbled back a step but caught himself. More of her spells came flying at him like bullets. Diego groaned and flung a palm out, and another burgundy cloud almost enveloped my aunt.

I heard Kennedy gasp as the blood left my face. This was too close. Without thinking, I fired off three deep orange bursts of flame that missed him by inches. When Diego's deadened eyes locked on mine, I realized I'd given away mine and Ken's location. My heart raced. Before he could focus again, Aunt Tara bowled him over with a cold gray mist. He stumbled and fell, before getting up again.

Sruthi ran quickly across the rocky cliff opposite us, and to my amazement I saw tree roots and vines floating along beside her. She held her hands in front of her and twirled them around, and I watched the vines fly down the cliff face and try to trap him in their grip. I could see the focus on her thin face, her teeth bared, as she tried to hold him through the earth. She glared down her long nose, chin held high, chest heaving. Her outfit billowed out behind her in a fierce wind that wasn't there moments before.

Eva, following her, slid to a stop near Sruthi and placed her fingers on her temples. In moments, the vines turned to chains. The faintest violet glow surrounded her and grew stronger the longer she stared at Diego. We watched him punch and kick at the air, and little wine-colored curses burst out of his palms every few seconds, but no matter how much he writhed, he was unable to break the bonds.

My aunt flexed her arms and sent more gray curses his way. A few hit him, and he bent over with a huff. But, spinning around, he appeared to catch the next few spells and twisted them in his hands before shooting them back at her in a red cloud. I saw her face the moment she realized what was happening; stunned, she was quickly enveloped too.

"No!" Kennedy screamed beside me, sending a dart the color of the sun right for Diego's heart.

My chest felt tight, like I couldn't breathe. I stumbled as I stood up. There was no one to protect us now. I met Ken's eyes and saw the realization hitting her too. We had to save our family, and there was no one left to do it but *us*. The girl gang.

I shut my eyes for a second and pictured the four of us shooting the movie scene where I played a girl showing up to war with her bow and arrow. I needed to channel that strength and courage. I drew my spine up straight and pushed my shoulders back. Channeling the voices of the thousands of strong, dark women who had been silenced before me rising up within my chest, I yelled, "Stop!" The earth trembled at my command and Diego looked up in shock.

"You will not get away with this," I heard from behind me. Stepping forward, my sister strode fiercely towards the edge of the cliff. And for the first time, I didn't try to stop her. I didn't try to protect her. Instead, I saw a lioness before me and I let her pass while she prepared her strike. Her curls blew out of her bun and the sun cast a beautiful golden highlight across her high cheekbones. Kennedy looked powerful. She didn't look like someone who was afraid of conflict anymore; she looked like someone who ended it. With three strong strides, she jumped off the side of the ridge and soared towards the valley floor. Yellow beams of light zigzagged from her outstretched palms as she rocketed down to the grass.

Eva jumped off the other edge and skirted the rocks, landing about halfway down the cliff face. From her twenty-foot high vantage point she kept her eyes trained on Kennedy, who was starting to glow as she walked forward.

"Let them go, *now*," she demanded. I could feel the strength in her high soprano.

Diego snorted, and with a final heave, the chains shattered in a million directions and with wide eyes I watched him draw back his arms. I overheard my sister whisper Sruthi's name through our orbs. Then, as another one of his clouds started to form, I felt wind whip my afro and caress my cheeks. Right before the sudden wall of air hit him, Sruthi pulled it to a stop, creating a barrier. Kennedy turned her brown eyes to Eva, who snapped her slim fingers and the transparent wall became dense rock.

I focused all of my energy on him, and with both hands outstretched, fired off burnt orange curses. Diego leapt into the air and grabbed the rock wall as two flames licked the ground where his feet had been. He shot a spell at me, which I avoided by inches.

When he aimed one at Sruthi, I saw Kennedy hit it in mid-air with one of her own golden rays of light. "Stop!" she yelled at him.

Eva sent bright violet balls rocketing towards him, and they slammed into the rocks around him, breaking off and tumbling to the ground. I ran along the cliff edge, closing the distance between myself and Diego and coming up above him.

My sister was ten feet from him, glowing a brilliant yellow like the sun. I had never seen her look so powerful before. Her curls stood up, her skin glistened, and her eyes gleamed. She was a fierce witch. Ken threw a curse the size of a soccer ball at him, hitting him squarely in the stomach. With a groan, he fell from the rock wall and onto the ground.

From above, Sruthi sent stones tumbling down onto Diego as Eva jumped the final twenty feet to the ground. Diego pulled himself shakily to his feet and glared at my friends, but he seemed to have lost track of me.

"Release them now," Kennedy ordered, still shimmering. "I don't want to be forced to kill you."

"Not a chance, child," he said menacingly, walking towards her. Pointing her right hand at him, she sent several yellow zaps directly at him, but he deflected them all.

"Why are you doing this?" she yelled throatily, radiating sun-kissed light.

Diego growled, "Power." Kennedy dove out of the way as several red curses came right for her. She jumped into the air and landed ten feet up on the cliffs weightlessly. Diego followed her, standing on a piece of stone jutting out from the wall. I saw my sister's eyes grow big with fear as he said, "You're no match for me, little girls." The orange glow around my hands grew bigger and bigger.

Sruthi threw her arms up in the air and twisted them above her head. Water from the falls whipped towards Diego, but he moved easily out of the way of the rushing water. She then twirled her fingers and the vines from earlier snaked around her, circling her. With grace, they lowered her to the valley floor and released her. One of Eva's spells caught Diego in the back and pounded him into the earth wall hard. We could all hear the huff that escaped his lungs. He turned towards Kennedy.

She locked eyes with me, and I knew what was coming. What I didn't know was whether her bright yellow shield would be strong enough to stop his red clouds. But I wasn't going to let anyone hurt my sister.

"What is power worth if you are all alone with it?" I yelled, enraged. Diving off the cliff, I felt my orange orb envelop me. I flew right at Diego, grabbing him from behind and spinning him out onto the field in a flame-colored tornado. We crashed into the ground in a trail of singed earth and the air left both of us. Kennedy flew to my side and helped me up, while Eva and Sruthi kept their palms trained on Diego. Then we grabbed each other's hands and squeezed.

"No one said we were a match," Kennedy growled at him.

"Match," I scoffed, still catching my breath.

"We're much stronger," Eva added, staring him down.

"Together," Sruthi breathed, smiling fiercely.

Tightly gripping each other's palms, once again orange and yellow met violet and green. The burst of light that slammed forward was enough to blow a section of the earth wall behind us to pieces and trap Diego against the parched grass. It was clear, yet solid; crystal, yet obsidian. My sister looked at me and nodded.

"Let them go!" I demanded, forcing my rough voice to be persuasive. The lilt of the siren seemed to take hold of Diego, and I saw a shiver run down his spine. "I demand that you release them all!"

He fought the urge to obey my command, and I watched the muscles in his arm ripple.

"You killed your own brother," my voice dropped to a low, compelling pitch. "Why are you trying to take so many lives? Release them *now*," I growled.

We watched Diego fight against our power. Another shiver ran down his spine. "I have... no... choice." He kept trying to break through our barrier of moving, shimmering light.

"We always have a choice," I told him, looking pointedly at my father.

"And you're making the wrong one," Kennedy's nostrils flared. My dad, aunt, and uncle looked like helpless dolls floating nearby.

His lips quivered slightly. Suddenly, resolve tightened in his eyes and they hardened to empty black stones. He drew his tan hands back with a shaky breath, and more clouds started to form in his palms. Eva was closest to Diego.

I felt our bond break as Sruthi whipped up more wind and sent it his way. She gritted her teeth and shoved with all her might.

"Eva!" I cried, "Watch out!"

Eva lifted her slim arms to her chest, but before she moved Diego froze, his eyes locked on her. "Eva?" he whispered, and then collapsed. Massive amounts of burgundy steam and smoke poured from his body, and it looked lifeless on the ground.

Kennedy shot me a wide-eyed look, and I raised my eyebrows. Eva's jaw dropped. *What the hell.*

To his left and right, my father, aunt, and uncle dropped to the ground in heaps.

8

Ivelisse

My mom appeared in a burst of red light. After making frantic eye contact with Kennedy and I, she ran to my father and got down on the ground beside him, pressing her luminescent hands to his chest. Her long braids were pulled back from her face, which was fierce with emotion as she worked to revive my dad with her healing powers.

Uncle Ben and Aunt Tara slowly sat up, holding their foreheads and looking around. My uncle stared at us, dumbstruck, and asked, "What just happened?"

Aunt Tara just looked up and beamed. "I *knew* you could do it." Then they reached over and embraced each other tightly. The sunlight ducked beneath the line of the trees, and everything was cast in a warm shadow.

My dad's eyes fluttered open and I fought the urge to run to him and wrap my arms around his neck. There was something to take care of first. I glanced over at Kennedy and saw that her face mirrored my thoughts.

The four of us strode closer to Diego, who was still laying on the ground. He was blinking and looking dazed and confused.

"Hold it right there," Kennedy commanded as he sat up, one hand held up in front of her.

"What- what's going on?" he asked. All of the anger and darkness was gone from his voice. His eyes searched each of our faces, and rested on Eva's last. "I-I-Ivelisse?"

Eva drew a deep, shaky breath. Her dainty features were stricken. "No one has called me that since…"

"Ivelisse!" Diego shouted, jumping to his feet. Mine and Kennedys' palms started to glow but we froze uncertainly. No one moved to stop him because his voice was filled with pure joy. "Ivelisse! Ivelisse!" He approached her slowly, arms held up in surrender, but his brown eyes were bright and emotional. "It's me, baby! Ivelisse! I can't believe it!"

Kennedy shot me another what-the-heck-is-going-on look and I shook my head and shrugged.

"D-dad?" her voice trembled as she pushed light brown hair out of her eyes. Her thick eyebrows mashed together. "That's impossible."

"I can't remember," he said, sinking to the ground in front of her. "I can't remember anything."

Kennedy turned to me and raised her eyebrows. "Can you help him?" She didn't lower her hands, ready to attack if I needed her to have my back.

Still in shock, I lowered myself to the ground so that I was kneeling beside him. I felt Sruthi's hand grip my shoulder and warmth coursed through my veins. I stared into his confused brown eyes for a moment, and started to whisper. "Tell me what happened."

He shook his head and pulled at the grass. "I can't remember." Frustration crept into his voice.

"Diego," I murmured, "tell me what happened to you." A warm breeze played with my afro. All of the anger and hatred that had consumed me minutes before transformed into confusion and a need to understand.

He was quiet for a minute, staring off into space. "It's coming back to me," Diego said quickly. "I think I was…I think I got cursed." He put his face in his hands.

"They said you were dead. You're dead," Eva whispered slowly from above me, hazel eyes wide with shock.

"What do you know about this curse?" My tone was silk and I held his gaze. I felt the others come to stand around us but I didn't break my focus.

"I got cursed," Diego whispered to himself, shaking his head. He looked up at Eva. "You broke the curse. I had to hear your name. Only then would I remember…" he said musically.

"Who cursed you?" I murmured, still staring into his eyes.

"My father," he said it like a question, eyebrows drawn together. I felt another hand on my shoulder; my dad. My heart skipped in my chest.

"Tell me about this curse," I said convincingly, my voice buttery.

Diego was silent again for just a moment, and then he looked back at me. When he spoke, his voice wavered. "My father grew sick and couldn't be cured. He was told he only had years left. He couldn't stand to see our legacy die out. He… he told me I had to get more power. Carry on the name. I refused." Tears filled his eyes. "Thirteen years ago."

I didn't blink. "Go on," I prodded. "Tell me what happened."

"He knew I was stronger than my brother," his voice was trance-like. "My father cursed me to leave the coven I'd married into and take his place in another coven when he couldn't lead anymore. He knew I wouldn't do that if I could remember my family," his voice broke. "And then when Antony stopped answering to him, he sent me here."

"Close your eyes," I said, and he did with a sigh. "Take a deep breath and see what you can remember."

"It's coming back to me in very small pieces," Diego replied.

"Keep breathing. Tell me what you see."

A few moments passed, and he looked up. His brown eyes weren't cold anymore, they were wide and heartbroken. "He made me take over his coven, which was far from my own. He faked my death so that I would have nothing to return to and made me lead under a new name. I remember fighting from the inside but not being able to do anything about it," his voice trembled.

"This was in Puerto Rico?"

"Yes." The waterfall continued to thunder behind him.

"Then what?" I asked quietly, still holding his gaze.

"Antony stopped answering to him, like I said. Started ignoring his orb, and leading his people down his own path. After years of this, my father grew impatient and angry and decided I had to come intervene and take charge over here. He resumed control of his coven in my absence."

"He made you kill your brother? His own son?"

Diego flinched and his face was drawn with pain. "Yes. And when your father showed up, he instructed me to take care of him as well. To protect his secret. I faked Antony's death near the river so no one would come looking over here and figure out what I'd done."

The fake signs of a scuffle we'd seen by the coven's base camp. I shut my eyes briefly, trying to slow my beating heart down.

"The dark magic I was trapped under was meant to absorb Antony's powers."

"The cloud?" I asked persuasively, but he looked confused.

"It looked like you were enclosing people in these red clouds."

Diego shook his head, "I can't remember."

With a shaky breath, Uncle Ben came to stand beside me. "I remember. I felt frozen. I could think, but my thoughts seemed slow. I just had to watch everything happening before me."

Aunt Tara nodded. "I can't imagine the long-term effects. It's frightening." Uncle Ben wrapped his arms around her. "That has to be why I couldn't find Cameron," she said about my father. "Why he didn't show up in anyone's orbs. Powerful magic."

My father cleared his throat and said somberly, "Some of the darkest witches and warlocks move to Puerto Rico to absorb the powers that come from being so close to the equator there. I am not surprised to hear another warlock is causing trouble," he took a deep breath. "Jada says it was only a night for me... but it felt like a very long, very deep sleep. At first, I could rationalize what was happening and try to think of ways to get out, but as time went on I grew more and more fatigued. I don't remember much after sunrise."

Uncle Ben looked at Diego. His jaw was set, but his eyes were soft. "I cannot imagine years of that. There would be absolutely no control. That is the darkest kind of magic I have ever seen."

Eva dropped to the ground beside me and reached out for her father's hand.

He looked deep into her eyes, so like his own. "The curse could only be broken if I heard your name," he murmured again.

"Every curse has a fail-safe," she said smartly, as if she were just reciting words from a book. I could see them mirrored in the arch to their noses, the thickness of their hair, the way they hesitantly smiled.

The light started to fade from his eyes. "What have I done, Ivelisse? How will you ever forgive me?"

It was my father who answered, his deep timber reassuring. "You lost your will when the curse was bestowed upon you. You've done nothing of your own free will. These are your father's actions, and he will pay the price for them." My father's face was grim.

Diego dropped his face into his palms again.

Everything around us had grown quiet and the tension had finally left our shoulders. I felt like I could breathe again, and I was happy to see Eva smiling uncertainly at her father in the dark. He still looked awed and shocked, but I was sure some time with his family would help bring more of his memories back. I glanced over at my sister, and was definitely not surprised to see her fingers looped through Sruthi's, a small smile on her face. Sruthi's dark eyebrows were question marks when she met my eyes, but I nodded solemnly, a grin tugging at my lips. I'd been waiting for them to figure it out.

I wrapped my arm around my dad's waist and squeezed, feeling immensely grateful that we had gotten here fast enough to save him. My aunt and uncle made promises to come see us soon, but my uncle had a coven to lead now.

As everyone said their goodbyes, Ken, Eva, and Sruthi came to stand by me. We grasped hands and smiled at each other, feeling exhausted but proud.

"Hey, Ken," I grinned, poking her in the ribs.

She shot little white sparks at me. "What?"

I raised my eyebrows, "Remember how you were complaining about not feeling useful?"

"Guess you really proved yourself wrong today," Sruthi said, smiling.

"What do you mean?" Ken's eyes were round as she looked from face to face.

Eva rolled her eyes. "*Chica*! You orchestrated that whole fight! You knew exactly who to call upon and when, and your fierce, feisty self is the reason we're not all in little red clouds."

"So much for *useless*," I murmured, wrapping my arm around her waist and hugging her.

"More like 'team leader," Eva said, getting in on the other side.

Sruthi enveloped us all in her slender arms, and I rested my tired head on someone's shoulder, feeling content.

Before I knew, everyone was standing in a circle joining hands. The light that formed around us was magnificent, and moments later our feet touched the ground back in Oregon. Tall pines swayed in a slight breeze, and dusk was settling in around the forest. The air was sweet and cold and fresh, and I'd never been happier to be *home*.

EPILOGUE

I turned in my applications for acting school. My parents aren't thrilled, but when you save your dad's life you kind of get a pass on things like moving away for college. Anyway, I think moving away for school will be great. My mom and I can talk through our orbs whenever my future roommate isn't around, and she'll definitely be less stressed about my being in the regular world as time goes on, as long as I come home for summer breaks. I'm still not allowed to use my powers outside of the coven, but, who knows? Maybe one day, when people like my sister are running our covens, we won't have to hide anymore. Maybe they'll make movies about us and accept us in their world. We can do a whole lot of good... I think we've shown that all you need is a little bit of girl power.

Look forward to _Girl Gang_: Coven II, featuring Sruthi's

story, next!